Eerie Elementary

Recess is a JUNGLE!

By Jack Chabert
Illustrated by Sam Ricks

BRANCHES

SCHOLASTIC INC.

READ ALL THE
Eerie Elementary
ADVENTURES!

 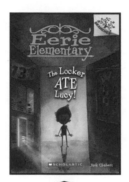 

MORE BOOKS
COMING SOON!

Table of Contents

For the wonderful teachers at Joshua Eaton Elementary School. Thanks for letting us play Tire Tower Tag, King of the Mountain, and Off the Wall. — JC

Text copyright © 2016 by Max Brallier
Illustrations copyright © 2016 Scholastic Inc.

Chabert, Jack, author.
Recess is a jungle! / by Jack Chabert ; illustrated by Sam Ricks. — First edition.
pages cm. — (Eerie Elementary ; 3)
Summary: At the end of recess at Eerie Elementary, everything on the school grounds suddenly comes alive and turns into a fog-filled jungle maze intent on trapping and disposing of hall monitor Sam Graves and his friends Antonio and Lucy.
ISBN 0-545-87352-5 (pbk. : alk. paper) — ISBN 0-545-87353-3 (hardcover : alk. paper) — ISBN 0-545-87364-9 (ebook) — ISBN 0-545-87366-5 (eba ebook) — 1. Elementary schools— Juvenile fiction. 2. Labyrinths—Juvenile fiction. 3. Best friends—Juvenile fiction. 4. Horror tales. [1. Schools—Fiction. 2. Labyrinths—Fiction. 3. Best friends—Fiction. 4. Friendship— Fiction. 5. Horror stories. 6. Horror fiction. gsafd] I. Ricks, Sam, illustrator. II. Title.
PZ7.C3313Re 2016
813.6—dc23 [Fic]
2015011352
ISBN 978-0-545-87353-6 (hardcover) / ISBN 978-0-545-87352-9 (paperback)

10 9 8 7 6 5 4 3 2   16 17 18 19 20

Printed in China   38
First edition, January 2016
Illustrated by Sam Ricks
Edited by Katie Carella
Book design by Will Denton

INTO THE WOODS . . .

"Power shot!" Sam Graves shouted as he kicked the soccer ball across the playground.

It was recess. Sam and his best friends, Antonio and Lucy, were passing a ball back and forth.

Antonio stopped the soccer ball with his foot just before it rolled beneath the swing set. He kicked it back to Sam.

"Pass to me!" Lucy shouted.

Sam kicked the ball to Lucy and then raced ahead. Mr. Nekobi, the old man who took care of Eerie Elementary, was raking leaves nearby. Sam waved at him as he darted past.

It was Mr. Nekobi who chose Sam to be the school's hall monitor. It was Mr. Nekobi who showed Sam what Eerie Elementary really was: a living, breathing thing that *fed* on students. The school was alive! And Sam Graves, the hall monitor, was now the protector of the school.

Just a month ago the school stage had tried to swallow Lucy and Antonio during the school play! Then, only days later, Sam and Antonio rescued Lucy after she was swallowed by her locker! Lucy and Antonio now knew the terrible truth about Eerie Elementary. And Mr. Nekobi had made them assistant hall monitors — so they could help Sam keep the other students safe.

Sam's thoughts were interrupted by the squawk of a crow. Big, black crows sat on the roof of the school. They usually gave Sam the willies. But not today. Sam ignored the birds and raced forward.

"Sam, incoming!" Lucy called out. The soccer ball soared through the air. Sam caught the ball with his foot and kicked it around the corner of the school.

Eerie Elementary looked like a castle made of crumbling, red bricks. The playground equipment was old and worn.

Sam dribbled the soccer ball around the huge wooden jungle gym. The jungle gym was full of tire swings and rope ladders and poles. It had a climbing net and a bright-red slide, too.

Sam was coming to the edge of the playground, where the soccer goal sat. A rusty fence surrounded the school. It stood just beyond the goal, covered in vines.

"Take the shot, Sam!" Lucy shouted.

Sam drew back his foot. He stared at the goal. Then he kicked the ball with everything he had!

POW!

The ball soared through the air and . . .

It missed the goal. It missed the goal by a lot. It bounced off the fence and rolled to a stop. The soccer ball rested against a huge knotted tree root that pushed up part of the fence. The ball was at the edge of a small wooded area beside the school.

Sam sighed. "I'm *so* bad at soccer!"

Lucy and Antonio caught up to Sam. Antonio slapped Sam on his back. "I'm sorry buddy, but it's true. Soccer is just not your sport."

FWEEE-IIIT!

A high-pitched whistle pierced the air. Sam's teacher, Ms. Grinker, stood at the school steps. "Recess is over!" she called. "Everyone inside now!"

Antonio tugged Sam's sleeve. "Your turn to get the ball, buddy," he said, pointing.

Sam felt a chill rush down his spine. As hall monitor, Sam could sometimes feel things that other students couldn't. And he felt something now. Something bad.

A moment later, the soccer ball began to roll. It moved entirely on its own. Sam, Antonio, and Lucy held their breaths. They were stunned. Very slowly, the soccer ball rolled through the twisted hole in the fence and into the dark woods . . .

AFTER IT!

2

Sam couldn't believe what he had just seen.

The ball was resting against that tree root, thought Sam. *And then it just started rolling! On its own!*

Ms. Grinker was hurrying the rest of the class into the school. Beside her was Mr. Nekobi. The old man caught Sam's eye. He gave Sam a slight nod. Sam knew what that meant: Mr. Nekobi wanted Sam to go into the woods after the ball.

"I'll get the ball," Lucy said. "I'm sure there's a reason it started to roll — maybe there's a little hill we can't see!"

"There's a reason, all right!" Antonio exclaimed. "Orson Eerie is the reason!"

Sam and his friends had learned that a mad scientist named Orson Eerie built Eerie Elementary more than a hundred years ago. But Orson Eerie found a way to live forever — he *became* the school.

ORSON EERIE 1871-?

Orson Eerie *was* Eerie Elementary.

"Come on, guys," Antonio said. "Forget about the ball."

Lucy wanted to go into the woods. Antonio didn't. The final choice was Sam's. Time was ticking!

Sam looked back. Mr. Nekobi was talking to Ms. Grinker. He was distracting her for them! *Perfect . . .*

"Okay, guys," Sam said. "We're going after that ball."

Lucy grinned. Antonio groaned. But together, the friends walked toward the fence. Pine trees towered over them.

They climbed through the twisted fence. Cool air rushed over them. They left the sunlight behind and entered the darkness of the woods.

"But what if *Orson Eerie* made the ball move?" Antonio asked.

"We're leaving school grounds," Sam said. "Orson Eerie has no power beyond this fence. We have nothing to worry about."

But as soon as Sam finished his sentence, a thick fog came from deep within the woods. In moments, it seemed to swallow them.

Sam couldn't see two feet from his face! He couldn't see his friends!

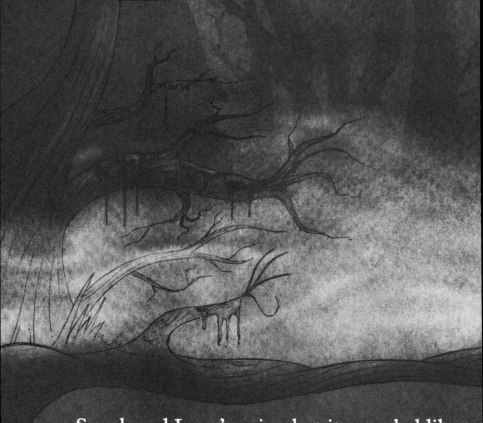

Sam heard Lucy's voice, but it sounded like she was miles away. He squinted. All he could see was thick, gray fog. All Sam could hear was swirling wind!

"Guys, where are you?!" Sam cried out. "Antonio! Lucy!"

Sam called again and again, but there was no response. His friends were gone!

SWAMP THING

3

Sam couldn't see a thing through the fog. He had no idea where the soccer ball was. And even worse — he had no idea where his friends were! He cupped his hands around his mouth and yelled as loud as he could. "Lucy! Antonio! Where are you?!"

Sam nearly tripped. The tree roots on the ground were uneven. It felt like they were trying to grab hold of him.

"HELP! SAM!"

Sam heard someone calling his name. It sounded like Lucy. He pushed his way through the fog and followed the sound of her voice. Lucy kept crying out, like she was in danger!

At last, Sam stumbled out of the fog. He could see again. But he couldn't believe his eyes: There was a large swamp in front of him.

Tree roots poked through the water. Dead branches floated on the surface. *A swamp? How could there be a swamp this close to school?* Sam thought. *It's like I'm in a wild jungle from a movie!*

Sam had never seen a swamp before in real life — and he knew there wasn't supposed to be one in these woods. Sam and Lucy had studied the school grounds in library books and in Orson Eerie's school blueprints. There wasn't a swamp *anywhere* in the town of Eerie!

"SAM! ANTONIO! HELP! HURRY!"
Lucy shouted again. Sam spotted Lucy on the
far side of the swamp.

One of the floating branches had grabbed
Lucy's backpack! Lucy was trying to wrestle
free, but she couldn't. The branch was dragging
her into the dark swamp! She quickly grabbed
hold of a thick log bobbing on the water.

"Hang on!" Sam shouted. "I'm coming!"

Sam's heart was pounding. *I need to get across the swamp to help Lucy!* he thought. *But if I step into the muddy water, I'll be pulled under, too.*

Suddenly, Sam felt something cold brush against his shoulder.

"AIIEEE!" he shrieked. Sam leapt back, thinking it was a snake. But it was just a long vine.

Sam had an idea.

He grabbed hold of the vine and gripped it tight. He eyed the monstrous swamp ahead of him. Sam gulped. He couldn't believe what he was about to do . . .

CRASH!

4

Sam got a running start and leapt. He clutched the vine as tight as he could as he swung out over the swamp.

"Lucy, duck!" Sam shouted. Sam swung over her head like Tarzan, the star of the old movies his dad loved. But Sam was no Tarzan. His fingers slipped from the vine and he crashed to the wet ground. **OOMF!** Sam scrambled to his feet. He had made it to the other side!

"Hurry, Sam!" Lucy cried out. The branch was tugging on her backpack, pulling her deeper into the swamp. If she let go of the log, she'd be dragged under in a second!

Sam yanked off his hall monitor sash and threw one end to Lucy. "Grab on!" Sam said. "I'll use this to pull you free!"

Lucy grabbed the sash. Sam used all his might to pull.

SCHLURP! Lucy ripped one foot from the muck and finally broke free from the branch's awful grasp. When Sam and Lucy were far enough away from the swamp, they collapsed.

"Wait!" Lucy cried. "Where's Antonio? He ran in the other direction. I heard him scream! He could be gone!"

Just then, there was an earsplitting crash. And another. It was coming from the pine trees up ahead!

"What are those n-n-noises?!" Lucy asked.

Sam had no idea.

The crash sounds grew louder and louder. Someone — or some*thing* — was coming toward them!

THE CROW

5

Sam and Lucy huddled together. The trees seemed to shake and the ground seemed to quake.

Lucy gasped, then shouted, "It's Antonio!"

Antonio raced out of the woods. His eyes lit up. "Guys! I found you!"

He fell at their feet. "I almost got eaten by a huge leaf! It was chomping at me like a mouth! Like **CHOMP! CHOMP! CHOMP!** I told you we were *crazy* to come looking for that soccer ball! It's just a ball — it's not worth getting eaten!"

"This shouldn't be happening! Not here!" Lucy exclaimed. "Orson Eerie's powers only work on school grounds."

"Yeah!" Antonio said. "And we're *definitely* not on school grounds! What's the deal?"

"It doesn't make any sense," Sam said. Had they been wrong about Orson Eerie? Did his strange powers work beyond the school? If they did, that meant the three of them would *never* be safe!

Sam looked around. The dark fog drifted between the trees. It was so thick that they couldn't even see the school. And the trees were the tallest Sam had ever seen. Vines and branches were twisted and tangled together.

This isn't the small forest that's usually next to the school, Sam thought. *It's a full-blown wild jungle! Orson Eerie must be to blame! And I don't see a way out . . .*

"Something's coming!" Antonio said.

Sam saw a small creature shuffling through the fog. Its feathery body was dark as night.

"A crow," Lucy said. "It's one of those huge crows that are always on the school roof."

The bird hopped toward them. Lucy and Antonio inched closer to Sam.

The crow finally came to a stop at their feet. The dark black bird looked up at Sam. Its silvery eyes seemed to stare right at him. No one said a word. They hardly breathed.

The sound burst from the crow's lungs. The crow flapped its wings and shot into the air. It circled around them three times. Then it darted into the fog, farther into the jungle.

"We should go after it," Sam said.

Antonio shook his head. "Not *again*! We should *not* follow *anything* farther into this creepy jungle!"

"But maybe the crow knows a way out," Lucy said.

Sam grinned. "Lucy's right. Come on!"

THE TOWERING MAN

6

The three friends chased after the crow. Then Antonio had an idea. "Wait a minute!" he said. He grabbed Sam's hall monitor sash and threw it around his waist. "Let's tie the sash around us so that we don't get separated again in this fog."

"Great idea!" Sam said.

Soon, they had the sash wrapped around them. Sam tied a knot in the front.

The crow swooped through the air.

They tried to chase after it, but it wasn't easy running in a group. The sash pulled and tugged at them. It was like they were trying to run with a Hula-Hoop around their waists.

Antonio bumped into Lucy. Lucy stepped on Sam's foot. Sam stumbled. They couldn't keep up with the crow!

The fog swirled around them.

"*Aww*, nuts!" Lucy said.

"Where'd that bird go?" Antonio asked.

The friends slowed to a walk and Sam loosened the sash. They continued through the strange jungle.

But it was no use. The crow was gone.

"Wait!" Antonio said. "What's that? Look up ahead."

Sam squinted. He saw the outline of the crow. But it wasn't flying. It wasn't moving at all. It seemed like it was frozen in midair.

The three friends stepped closer.

The fog thinned out.

Sam and Antonio and Lucy stopped dead in their tracks.

The crow wasn't frozen in midair. It was standing on someone's shoulder. The shoulder of a huge, towering man.

THE STATUE'S FACE

7

The huge, towering man did not move. Neither did the crow. Fog swirled around them. Very slowly, Sam inched forward. The hall monitor sash tugged at Lucy and Antonio to follow him.

There was a gust of cool wind and the fog cleared. They saw, then, that it was not a man. Not really.

"It's just a statue!" Lucy exclaimed.

Antonio breathed a sigh of relief. "We were worried over a big hunk of stone!"

The statue was cracked and chipped. Large black insects crawled in and out of it. Green moss covered much of the statue, including its face. The statue stood atop a stone base covered in vines.

"The soccer ball!" Antonio said, pointing. The ball rested against the base of the statue.

"Hey, we found it!" Lucy said.

Antonio scooped it up and wiped mud off of it.

Sam barely heard his friends. He was too busy staring at the statue. He wondered who the man was . . .

SQUAWK! SQUAWK! The crow flapped its wings and flew into the fog.

Sam untied the sash and threw it over his shoulder. "Can you two help me up?" he said. "I want to peel away that slimy green gunk, so we can see the statue's face."

Moments later, Lucy stood on Antonio's shoulders. And Sam was climbing up Lucy's back. Antonio groaned. "You guys, how strong do you think I am?"

"Pretty strong!" Sam said with a grin. "Just hold still for one more second."

Antonio stumbled a bit, but Lucy held tight to Sam's ankles. Sam grabbed on to the top of the statue. They were steady, now. Sam's fingers clutched the moss. Slowly, he began pulling it off the statue's face.

The moss was wet, and cold as ice. It smelled of mud and earth. As Sam peeled it away from the statue's mouth, he felt cold air rush at him. It was like something old and lifeless had just breathed on him.

Sam gulped. He continued peeling away the moss. At last, a large bit came free. Sam saw a face staring back at him. He cried out, "The st-st-statue . . . it's a statue of Orson Eerie!"

IT'S A TRAP!

8

Sam was clinging to the statue. Lucy looked up at him. "Orson Eerie? All the way out here in the jungle?" she asked.

The thought of the creepy scientist made Antonio's legs feel wobbly. He stumbled and Lucy fell forward. Sam tumbled from her shoulders. A second later, they all collapsed on the ground in a heap.

Something caught Antonio's eye. He pulled at the vines covering the statue's base. There was writing on the stone.

THIS STATUE MARKS THE PURCHASE OF PROPERTY BY ORSON EERIE IN THE YEAR 1917

"*Hmm,*" Lucy said. "I wonder . . ."

"What?" Sam asked.

Lucy unzipped her backpack and pulled out Orson Eerie's journal. Sam and Antonio had found the red leather book when they went into the depths of the school to rescue Lucy. She quickly flipped the pages.

"Look at this map!" Lucy cried out. "I think Orson Eerie bought this land for the school! See the area marked SOCCER FIELD?"

Land I bought for
Eerie Elementary:
PLAYGROUND
SCHOOL
BUILDING

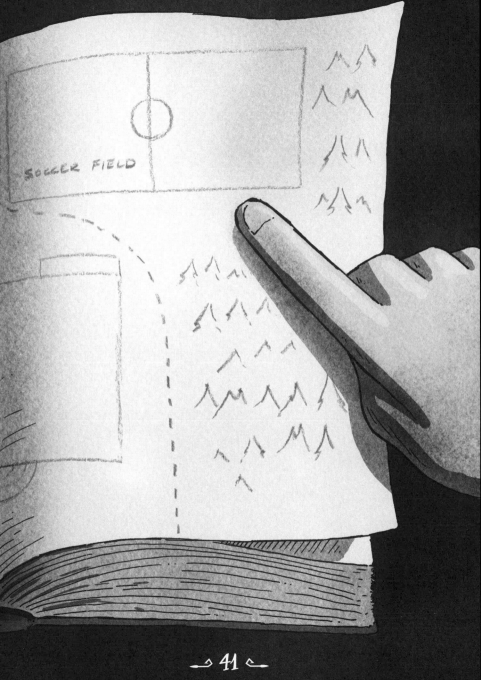

SOCCER FIELD

"But a soccer field was never built," said Antonio. "These trees were never knocked down! And the fence was never even moved!"

Sam gulped. He had a horrifying thought. "Maybe *anything* that's tied to the school is alive! Maybe it's *all* under Orson Eerie's spell! His power . . . It could reach farther than we ever imagined!"

Sam looked up at the stone face. It almost looked like it was grinning! Sam swallowed.

"We really need to find a way back to school," Lucy said. "We've been away for too long."

Lucy's words made Sam's blood run cold. Sam felt the hall monitor sash in his hands. He looked at the soccer ball and then up at the towering statue. Suddenly, it all made sense. *Terrifying sense.*

"We left the students unprotected!" Sam exclaimed. "While we've been stuck in this jungle, Eerie Elementary has been left without its protectors! Without *us*! Orson Eerie pulled that ball in here so we'd follow it!"

Lucy couldn't believe it. "Do you mean we've been tricked?"

"Yes!" Sam said. "This was all just a trap!"

"And with us lost in this jungle," Antonio said, "the school is free to attack the students!"

HURRY!

"We need to get back to school NOW!" Sam cried. He was just able to spot the school through the fog. The top of the building peeked above the trees.

"That way!" Lucy said. They raced through the woods. The trees seemed to howl. The branches rattled and the leaves shook.

Sam's heart pounded. His legs hurt. He had never run so hard in his life.

"We're getting close! I can see the fence!" Antonio said.

They scampered up a small hill. At last, they crawled through the fence and burst out of the thick jungle.

They now found themselves back on the playground, standing next to the swing set. Up ahead were the slides, then the monkey bars. And just beyond that, the school. Fog surrounded it.

Sam caught his breath. He thought, *This afternoon was crazy scary, but now we're safe —*

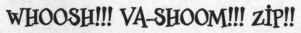

WHOOSH!!! VA-SHOOM!!! ZIP!!

The bright-green playground grass was suddenly sprouting up all around them. It was growing out of control. Sam, Lucy, and Antonio stumbled.

"What's happening?!" Lucy screamed.

Huge blades of grass shot up. One whizzed past Sam's head. Each blade was ten feet high!

The friends huddled together. Then, all of a sudden, everything stopped. Grass had grown up around them. Ahead of them was a long, winding path through the greenery.

Sam's eyes were as wide as silver-dollar pancakes. "Um," he said, "did our playground just turn into a *hedge maze*?"

They looked around. Sam was right. They were standing in the middle of a winding labyrinth with walls of grass and trees.

"We'll never get out of here!" Lucy said.

"We *have* to find a way out," Sam said.

Antonio grinned and reached into his pocket. "Have no fear! I've got my lucky peanut butter and jelly sandwich! I'll leave a trail of breadcrumbs!" he said. "That way, even if we get *totally* lost, we can at least get back to where we started."

Sam smiled. "Good thinking! Now, come on — through the hedge maze we go!"

THROUGH THE HEDGE MAZE

10

The walls of the hedge maze towered over Sam and his friends.

"Going through this maze is the only way back to school," Sam said.

"And if this whole swamp-maze thing was a trap from the start, we really need to *hurry*!" Lucy said.

"The monkey bars are on the far side of the playground," Antonio said. "They're right next to the school's rear steps."

"So we need to go toward the monkey bars!" Sam said. "Come on!"

The friends began to follow the winding path. Antonio dropped breadcrumbs as they walked. The dark maze snaked through the playground! Sam saw the same things he had seen during recess — the swings and the slides — but everything was different now.

Grassy walls surrounded the playground equipment. The ground was mucky and wet. Vines crawled over everything.

Rocking horses seemed to cry out as Sam walked past. Their springs squeezed and their eyes bulged.

A merry-go-round,
covered in vines,
spun on its own. It
creaked and howled
with each turn.

Finally, Sam spotted the monkey bars. "We're almost to the steps!"

"But getting there won't be easy," Lucy said.

Lucy was right. There was now a swamp below the monkey bars! It covered the entire path. There was no way around it.

"Maybe we can swim across the swamp?" Antonio asked.

"The last swamp almost ate me!" Lucy said.

"Maybe this one is different . . ." Antonio said.

"Lucy," Sam said. "Do you have anything in your backpack you don't need?"

Lucy opened her backpack. She dug past her school books and sunglasses and pulled out her neon yellow pencil case.

Sam took the case. "Let's see how the swamp reacts if we throw this in."

He tossed the pencil case into the swamp. It splashed onto the muddy water and floated on top. Suddenly, a long, winding branch burst through the muddy surface. The branch grabbed the case and dragged it below.

Sam, Lucy, and Antonio all gulped. "Nope," Lucy said. "This swamp's not any different."

"Then there's only one way across," Sam said, stepping up. He reached out and grabbed hold of a bar. It was covered in vines and moss.

Sam took a deep breath. "I'll go first," he said.

Then he began to climb.

MONKEYING AROUND

11

Sam was out to the third bar when he looked down. The swamp below bubbled and burped. Muddy water splashed Sam's sneakers. Tree limbs reached out for him.

Sam's hands were sweaty. *There's no way I'll make it across without falling!* he thought. *But I have to!*

Sam was halfway when Lucy began to climb. Antonio was the last to cross. "I've always hated the monkey bars!" he groaned.

As Sam got close to the end, the monkey bars began to shake. The metal creaked and moaned.

"Hold on tight!" Sam shouted.

"It's trying to shake us off!" Lucy yelled.

The structure swayed from side to side.

Sam swung for the next bar — there was only one to go until the end. Just then, Lucy shrieked.

The monkey bars shot up into the air! The three friends held on tight.

Sam gasped. *We're twenty feet up in the air!* he thought.

Slippery vines had crawled up the monkey bars. One long vine wrapped itself around Sam's hand. His fingers were being *lifted* from the bar! "I can't hold on much longer!" he yelled.

The vine plucked Sam's pinkie finger and he lost his grip. He was plummeting down, toward the monstrous swamp. At the last second, Sam grabbed on to Lucy's jeans. He clutched the fabric as tight as he could.

SCHLURP! The swamp water bubbled up. The monkey bar set began sinking back down. Sam's stomach did a flip as everything dropped. The swamp was about to swallow the monkey bars!

Lucy gritted her teeth. Only one bar left. Using all her might, she reached out and grabbed it. Sam was able to scramble onto the bottom rung. Together, he and Lucy narrowly escaped. But Antonio was still making his way across.

The metal bars dipped in the middle. Antonio's feet hung closer to the swamp. Mud splashed his legs.

"Faster, Antonio!" Sam called.

"I'm trying!" Antonio cried out. "I don't want to be swamp food!"

He quickly swung from bar to bar. The metal howled as he dove off the monkey bars. He crashed to the ground beside his friends.

KER-SPLOOSH!

The three friends looked back just in time to see the swamp swallow the entire monkey bar set!

Sam raced ahead. *We're so close!* he thought.

His heart was pounding. He expected to run straight through this last bit of maze and see the rear steps of the school. He expected to make it *back* in time to stop Orson Eerie from attacking the students. He expected this horrible day to be over!

Sam ran as fast as he could. Antonio and Lucy were hot on his heels. But then he began to panic. He was looking at *the swing set*!

"No!" Sam cried out. "We're back at the beginning!"

Lucy hung her head. "This really is a maze. And we're trapped. It's hopeless."

"It's not *totally* hopeless," Antonio said. "Luckily I dropped those breadcrumbs as we went! They'll show us where we've already been. So we can take a different way out!"

But then Antonio stopped. The ground was bare. "Wait a minute — they're gone!"

IS THERE ANY WAY OUT?

12

A ntonio looked at the empty path. "Who took my PB&J crumbs?!" he exclaimed.

Sam's heart was pounding. His eyes darted across the ground. "Crumbs can't have just disappeared!"

"It's not possible . . ." Lucy said. Her hands were trembling.

SQUAWK!

The friends spun around. The huge crow from before landed on the seesaw. A piece of bread dropped from its mouth.

"That crow must have eaten *all* the breadcrumbs!" Sam said. The bird flapped its wings and shot into the air.

Lucy kicked at the damp ground. "It's like everything is working against us."

Sam plopped down on the seesaw. "I'm afraid we'll never get out of this maze."

Suddenly, one end of the seesaw *jumped*! "Whoa!" Sam shrieked. The seesaw jumped again. It was alive, too! Sam tumbled off.

Sam sat up. He was covered in mud. But he was smiling. "That's it!" he said. "I know *exactly* how to find our way out of here."

"You do?" Antonio asked.

"I think so . . ." Sam said. "Can you guys pin down this seesaw?"

"Wrestle a monstrous seesaw?" Antonio said, rolling up his sleeves. "Bring it on!"

Lucy and Antonio jumped on the seesaw, pinning one side to the ground. The seesaw jerked and jumped.

"Hurry, Sam!" Antonio said. "We can't hold this thing down forever!"

Sam quickly climbed up and stood on the other end of the rusty seesaw. It quaked. Sam was barely able to grip the cold metal handle. It was like he was surfing!

"It's working!" Sam said.

"Less talking, more looking!" Antonio said. The seesaw was trying its hardest to fling Lucy and Antonio off.

Finally, Sam managed to stand up straight. From where Sam stood, he could see the whole hedge maze. The strange labyrinth wrapped all the way around Eerie Elementary. But Sam smiled. "I can see it! I can see the way out!"

THE HORROR!

13

From his spot, Sam could see the zigzagged path they would need to take to escape the maze. He tried to take a picture of every twist and turn with his mind. They needed to take a left after the swings, a right before the tetherball, continue past the slides, and then take a final right after the merry-go-round. Then they'd finally be at the school steps!

"We can do this!" Sam cried. "Let's go!"

"We'll be out of this creepy-crawly maze in no time!" Antonio said.

The three friends raced through the maze. Eerie Elementary knew that Sam and his friends were close to escaping. The monstrous school did everything it could to stop them. Vines lashed out at them. The ground became wet and mucky. Sam, Lucy, and Antonio just kept running.

"Left!" Sam called out as they raced past the howling swings.

"Next right!" Sam shouted as they dove beneath the whirling tetherball.

"Around this corner!" Sam yelled as they dashed past the merry-go-round.

Finally, they were out. They burst free from the maze. The school steps were just ahead of them.

"We did it!" Lucy shouted. "We escaped!"

The steps were just a few feet away. But what Sam saw next almost made his heart stop.

The entire jungle gym had come to life! The huge wooden and plastic structure was as tall as a house — and it was marching toward the school.

Sam gulped. He had been right: Orson Eerie *had* led Sam and his friends into the swamp on purpose — to distract them from his REAL plan. Orson Eerie was going to use the jungle gym to march inside the school! He was going to feast on students!

İT'S ALİVE!

14

Wooden stakes jabbed at the ground as the monstrous jungle gym stomped toward the school. It moved like a spider.

Sam looked up. Fog surrounded Eerie Elementary. No one would be able to see the jungle gym! No one would know about the horror just outside their walls!

The jungle gym raised one giant stake and jabbed it into the school.

WHACK!!!

Sam gasped. Everyone inside was in terrible danger. He had to act now!

"Hey, Orson!" Sam shouted at the jungle gym. "Before you snack on *those* students, you've got a hall monitor to deal with!"

The jungle gym stopped moving. Slowly, it turned.

Sam shivered. The jungle gym seemed to have a *face* — and it was staring directly at Sam. The long red slide was like a tongue. Above the tongue was a mouth framed in wood.

Suddenly, a tire swing swung out at Antonio. He screamed as the tire dropped onto him. It quickly tightened its grip — like a huge rubber belt.

"It's got me!" he cried out.

Lucy and Sam raced toward their friend. A climbing pole ripped from the ground and swung at them. "Watch out!" Lucy shouted, as they dove to the ground.

WHOOSH! The metal pole swung over their heads.

Sam and Lucy scrambled to their feet.

Lucy shrieked. The jungle gym's climbing net had gotten ahold of her! The net yanked her up into the air. She was like a fly caught in a spider's web.

Sam stumbled back. *This freaky jungle gym just grabbed both of my friends!* he thought. *How will I stop this thing!?*

Sam's mind raced. He thought back to how he defeated Eerie Elementary when it attacked during the school play. He had tossed a huge tub of peanut butter into its mouth to stop it from chomping Antonio.

It's like each horrible creature is a part of Orson Eerie himself! Sam thought.

His eyes darted around. He spotted the soccer ball lying at Antonio's feet.

Can I do it? Sam asked himself. *Can I do what I'm terrible at? Can I use the very thing that got us into this mess to save us? Only one way to find out . . .*

"Antonio!" Sam called. "Kick the ball to Lucy!"

"You want to play soccer *now*?" Antonio cried out.

"You bet I do!" Sam yelled.

The tire swing squeezed Antonio's waist. He could barely move!

At last, Antonio managed to kick the ball. It flew toward Lucy.

"Lucy!" Sam called. "The soccer ball! Over to me!"

The climbing net was lifting Lucy way up and dropping her down — like a yo-yo. She groaned and reached out, fighting against the net. Finally, she was able to grab the ball! She flung it to Sam.

The mad jungle gym roared. One leg lifted up, ready to *crush* the ball . . .

A FINAL KICK

15

The monstrous jungle gym's wooden leg just missed the soccer ball! It slammed into the muddy ground. Sam stopped the ball with his foot.

The jungle gym stomped toward Sam.

SCHMACK!

SQUASH!

SMUSH!

The jungle gym's slide rolled out like a long red carpet. It snaked around, lashed out, and smacked the ground at Sam's feet.

"Kick the ball, Sam!" Lucy shouted.

"Hurry! I c-c-can't breathe!" Antonio called.

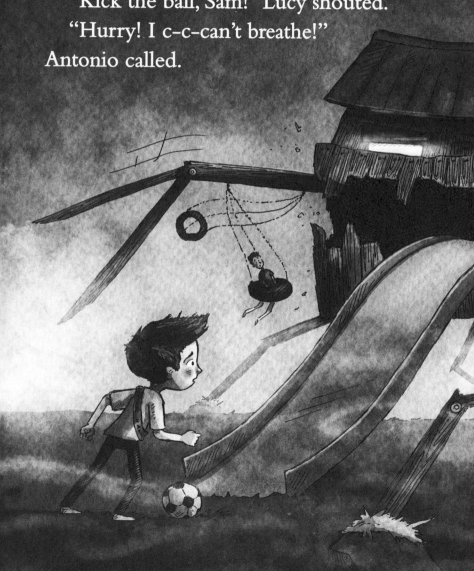

The wooden mouth above the slide was chomping open and closed. Wood splintered with every bite. Sam could tell that the school wanted to scoop him up with the tongue and swallow him whole.

This is the moment! Sam thought.

Sam pulled back his foot, eyed the soccer ball, and —

The ball soared through the air! It whizzed above the tongue. An instant later, the ball disappeared. It had flown directly into the monstrous jungle gym's mouth!

"DIRECT HIT!" Antonio cried out.

"NICE SHOT!" Lucy screamed.

Sam caught his breath. For one moment, everything was quiet.

Then the jungle gym stumbled from side to side. The two windows above the slide bulged like eyes. The legs shook. The wood cracked. A long moan escaped from its mouth. The giant tongue slide flopped around. The monster was choking! It lurched forward, toward Sam.

Sam stepped back.

And then, all at once, the huge structure became lifeless. The tire around Antonio loosened. The climbing net dropped Lucy to the ground. The wood settled. Even the fog began to clear.

"Not bad for someone who's *terrible* at soccer," Antonio joked.

But before Sam could reply, there was a

KLANG!

THE STRANGEST SCHOOL

16

The school doors flew open. "Sam! Lucy! Antonio! Where have you been?" Ms. Grinker yelled from the top of the stairs. Mr. Nekobi stood beside her. He had a slight grin on his face.

"Recess ended thirty minutes ago!" Ms. Grinker continued.

Thirty minutes ago? Sam thought. *It feels like we were gone a lot longer than that!*

"I'm sorry, Ms. Grinker," Sam said. "We got lost in the fog."

Ms. Grinker frowned. "What fog?" she asked, looking around. "Anyway, a little fog shouldn't keep you from getting to class. Especially not if you all want to continue being hall monitors!"

Ms. Grinker stopped as she turned to go back inside. She eyed the jungle gym. "Hey . . ." she said. "Didn't the jungle gym used to be over there?"

"Oh no, Ms. Grinker," Mr. Nekobi said. "It was being moved today. Didn't you get my note?"

Ms. Grinker glared. "No. I didn't."

Sam and Lucy and Antonio giggled.

"Enough laughing!" she barked. "You three, come inside! And wipe your feet — somehow you got covered in mud!"

Ms. Grinker shook her head. Then the two adults stepped back inside.

Lucy looked down at her clothes. "She's right. We *are* a mess, aren't we?"

Antonio chuckled. "Well, we *did* just hike through a wild jungle!"

"And we braved a hedge maze full of monstrous playground stuff!" Sam added.

Sam looked around. He looked at the playground. He looked at the woods beyond the playground.

Sam swallowed. "Lucy, Antonio," he said. "Orson Eerie is much stronger than we ever imagined. His powers go past the regular school grounds."

Lucy nodded. "I'll look closely at Orson Eerie's journal to find anything I might have missed before. Who knows where else his powers reach . . ."

Antonio threw his arms around his friends' shoulders. "Let's worry about that tomorrow," he said. "For the rest of the day, I just want to relax. No monster jungle gyms, no hedge mazes, and hopefully no homework! Please tell me tomorrow is Saturday!"

"Um, Antonio," Lucy said, chuckling. "Tomorrow is *Tuesday*."

Antonio groaned. "*Of course* this mess happened on a Monday!"

The three friends laughed, and then began walking toward the stairs.

WHOOSH!

Sam turned in time to see the soccer ball bouncing down the jungle gym slide. It rolled to a stop at Sam's feet.

Sam slowly and carefully bent down and picked it up. He smiled with relief — it was just a regular old ball now. Sam tucked it under his arm, and together he and his friends walked back into the strangest school anyone had ever known: Eerie Elementary.

Jack Chabert was a hall monitor at Joshua Eaton Elementary School in Reading, Massachusetts. But unlike our hero, Sam Graves's, school, Jack's school was *not* alive. Jack was pleased to make it through elementary school without ever getting lost in a monstrous playground hedge maze.

Today, Jack Chabert monitors the halls of a different building: a strange, old apartment building in New York City that he calls home. His days are spent playing video games, eating junk food, and reading comic books. And at night, he walks the halls, always prepared for the moment when his building will come alive.

Sam Ricks went to a haunted elementary school, but he never got to be the hall monitor. As far as he knows, the school never tried to eat him. Sam graduated from The University of Baltimore with a master's degree in design. During the day, he illustrates from the comfort of his non-carnivorous home. And at night, he reads strange tales to his four children.

HOW MUCH DO YOU KNOW ABOUT

Eerie Elementary

Recess is a JUNGLE?

Why does Sam think it is safe to follow the soccer ball?

What do Sam and his friends discover when they follow the crow?

Antonio drops PB & J crumbs to keep from getting lost. Does it work? Why or why not?

Orson and Sam are enemies. Write part of the story from Orson's point of view instead of Sam's.

Sam carefully explains how to escape the hedge maze. Work with a partner to write out instructions to do something such as playing soccer, walking to school, or escaping a maze!

scholastic.com/branches